THE TRANSFORMERS
MORE THAN MEETS THE EYE!

CAR SHOW BLOW UP

Written by Dana Rosenfeld Illustrated by Earl Norem

AUTOBOT **DECEPTICON**

MARVEL BOOKS

It was late afternoon in the Autobot city called Metroplex. The Autobots were finishing up their day's work.

"What a long day this has been," complained Hoist, sitting down heavily beside the Autobot leader Ultra Magnus. "My energy reserves feel drained."

Ultra Magnus laughed. "You'll be fine, Hoist. Everyone should work at least once a day."

WHOOSH! Hot Rod raced past Ultra Magnus. Close behind him was the veteran Autobot, Kup.

"What's going on?" Ultra Magnus yelled over the roar of their engines.

Hot Rod was so excited he could hardly talk. "There's a car show at the coliseum tonight," he told Ultra Magnus. "We heard about it on our car radios. They will be showing a robot car that can follow voice commands. Kup and I are going to check it out."

Shadows began to fall along the hillside outside the Autobot city. They hid a terrible sight within their darkness. Galvatron, cruel leader of the Decepticons, and a few of his warriors were spying on the Autobot city.

"Look at that city," growled Galvatron. "They harvest energy from many sources down there. That means they don't have to steal fuel like we do. We waste too much time stealing fuel. The time we spend stealing would be better spent waging war on the Autobots."

"Quite true, great leader," said Starscream. "Why not build a city of your own?"

"No!" Galvatron screamed. "We can't spare any Decepticons to do that kind of work. I need them all to fight. I must force others to build me a city! But who would be capable of such a feat?"

As Galvatron talked to Starscream about having a city of his own built, his communication expert Soundwave was tuning into the conversations down in the Autobot city.

Soundwave had the best hearing in the world. He could hear a fly sneeze or a mosquito cough. He overheard Hot Rod tell Ultra Magnus about the car show and the special robot car. He told Galvatron what he had overheard.

"A robot car, eh?" Galvatron muttered. "That gives me an idea."

Galvatron turned to his warriors. "We will steal the robot car, rip apart its circuitry and use it to create an army of robots who will build Decepticon City for me. That's what I need, robots so simple that they do not question my orders, but do as they're told—a race of slave robots!"

"Wheeeee!" Hot Rod sang as he raced toward town. "Come on, Kup! I'm beating you!"

"This is not a race," Kup snapped. "Honestly! Why do you have to make everything a game?"

ZOOM! Kup's words were drowned out by the roar of engines overhead.

It was the evil Decepticons flying into town! Hot Rod and Kup skidded to a stop in front of the Coliseum just in time to see the Decepticons change into their warrior forms and creep into the building.

"I don't like the look of this," said Hot Rod.

"Neither do I," agreed Kup, transforming into robot mode. "You go warn the others while I stay here and try to see what's going on. I'll catch up with you as soon as I can."

"Why can't *I* stay?" Hot Rod cried. "I'd stay out of trouble."

"No you wouldn't" said Kup sternly. "Now scoot!"

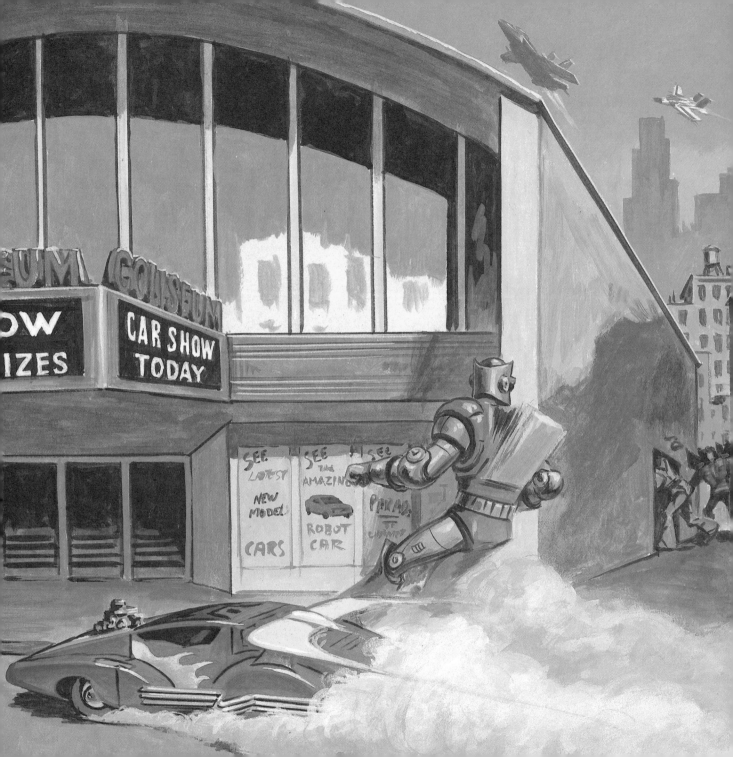

As soon as Hot Rod turned around, Kup sneaked into the coliseum. It was cool and dark inside. He stayed close to the walls so the Decepticons wouldn't see him.

"Find the fuse boxes that control the lights," Kup heard Galvatron order. "If we're lucky, we can knock out the fuses and cause a blackout during the show. Then we can steal the robot car while everyone's in the dark!"

Kup peered around the corner to see Galvatron and his warriors yanking open a row of electrical boxes.

"Found it!" Rumble shouted.

"Uh-oh," Kup thought. "I'd better catch up with Hot Rod and the others and tell them to get down here—right away!"

Kup was in such a hurry to get outside that he didn't see Starscream until it was too late.

CRUNCH!!! Starscream's powerful hands came down on Kup's back and lifted him into the air.

"What have we here?" sneered the Decepticon. "Why, it's a scruffy little Autobot. Old, too," he said. "You need a little polishing up. Looking a little moldy."

"Really, now," said Kup. "I may not be the youngest Autobot around, but I don't steal cars, like you rotten Decepticons are planning to do."

"Galvatron!" Starscream yelled as he carried Kup to the Decepticon leader. "Look what I found! An Autobot spy!"

"A *spy*?" said Galvatron. "Ahhh, it's old Kup. How much of our plan have you heard, Kup?"

Kup said nothing.

"Won't talk, eh?" said Galvatron. "Very well. Starscream, tie him up so he can't escape. We'll take him back to headquarters after we've stolen the robot car."

Ultra Magnus! ULTRA MAGNUS!"
Hot Rod screeched to a stop in front of the surprised Autobot leader.

"What happened?" Ultra Magnus asked as the other Autobots rushed to the scene. "Where's Kup?"

"The Decepticons are all over the coliseum!" Hot Rod gasped. He had driven so fast that he was out of breath. "I left Kup there to see what was going on. He was supposed to catch up with me but he's nowhere in sight. Something must have happened. Oh, I should never have left him there!"

"Don't worry, Hot Rod," said Ultra Magnus. "We'll find him. Autobots, transform! We're going to rescue old Kup!"

"But hurry!" said Hot Rod. "The car show starts in less than an hour!"

Back at the coliseum, Galvatron paced back and forth impatiently as Rumble worked on the electrical wiring.

"All set!" said Rumble, twisting one last piece of wire and closing the fuse box. "Just pull this thing here and all the lights will blow. Poof! Surprise! All dark."

"Great!" said Galvatron. He rubbed his hands together and laughed. "And just in time! Here come the cars now!"

A burst of music signaled the beginning of the show. Kup watched from the corner where he was tied up.

"Look at all those people!" he thought. "If only I could warn them! But wait! Those aren't any old cars! Those are the Autobots!"

In came the Autobots! The Decepticons were too excited about their fuse box to look at the line of cars that was rolling into the ring below. People watching were very impressed.

"Look at the neat car, Mom!" said a little girl, pointing to Bumblebee. "He's just my size!"

"*Well*!" said Bumblebee to himself. "I didn't think I was *that* small!"

Tracks was following Bumblebee. He laughed. "Don't you wish you looked more like me?" he teased. "Being a sleek piece of metal like me does make life easier sometimes."

"Quiet!" Hot Rod commanded in a whisper. "This is a rescue mission, not a beauty contest!"

Ultra Magnus was nervous. None of the Autobots had seen the Decepticons or Kup, and he didn't know what the Decepticons planned to do—or when.

"Keep your eyes open," he whispered to his warriors. "And get ready to transform when I give the word."

"Ladies and gentlemen," a voice boomed over the sound system. "Welcome to our all-new car show!"

"Get ready," Galvatron snapped at his warriors. "As soon as we pull the switch, all of you go into action. Starscream will swipe the robot car while we sneak around back."

Kup was struggling to break the bonds that held him. "If only I could tell the Autobots where the Decepticons are!" he thought.

"And now the moment we've all been waiting for!" the booming voice said. "The amazing robot car!"

"Pull the switch!" screamed Galvatron as he ran towards the fuse box.

"It's now or never," thought Kup, and stuck his foot right in front of Galvatron.

CRASH!!! The audience gasped as the Decepticon leader smashed through the glass window and fell through the air towards the arena below!

THUD!!! Galvatron landed in a heap right in front of Ultra Magnus.

"Oof!" said Galvatron.

"Autobots transform!" Ultra Magnus yelled, putting on his brakes. "Autobots transform!"

The Autobots didn't have to be told twice. By the time Galvatron had struggled to his feet, the Autobots had transformed and were standing around him. Galvatron was their prisoner!

"Ultra Magnus!" cried Kup from the glass booth. "They're up here! They want to steal the robot car!"

"There he is!" Hot Rod cried. "Don't worry, Kup! We're on our way!"

The Decepticons didn't know what to do. The Autobots had captured their leader, but *they* had one of the Autobots. "Don't try anything funny!" Starscream called out to the Autobots. "We've got your scruffy friend prisoner. Make one move and he's history!"

"Autobots, stay where you are!" said Ultra Magnus. "We don't want Kup to get hurt!"

"Forget that," Hot Rod said to himself as he sneaked off in Kup's direction. "Kup needs me."

"You've got ten seconds to let our leader go," Starscream yelled to the Autobot leader. "Or we start firing!"

"Oh, no!" Kup thought. "All those people!"

"Ten," said Starscream. "nine…eight…seven…"

Suddenly, Kup felt his hands being freed. It was Hot Rod! Kup was free!

"Geronimo!" yelled Hot Rod as he and Kup dove into the arena. Taken by surprise, the Decepticons forgot to fire. But the Autobots didn't! Within minutes, the Decepticons were running for their lives and the audience and the robot car were safe.

"Victory for the Autobots!" yelled Ultra Magnus.

"Except for one thing," said Kup as he limped up to his leader. "Galvatron escaped."

"He'll be back," said Ultra Magnus. "Don't worry."

"And we'll be ready for him," said Kup. "Right, Hot Rod?"

Hot Rod smiled. "Right!"